Dangerous Trainers

SUSAN GATES

Illustrated by Martin Remphry

BRITISH
INTERNATIONAL
SCHOOL VIETNAM

OXFORD
UNIVERSITY PRESS

OXFORD

UNIVERSITY PRESS

Great Clarendon Street, Oxford OX2 6DP

Oxford University Press is a department of the University of Oxford.
It furthers the University's objective of excellence in research, scholarship,
and education by publishing worldwide in

Oxford   New York

Auckland   Cape Town   Dar es Salaam   Hong Kong   Karachi
Kuala Lumpur   Madrid   Melbourne   Mexico City   Nairobi
New Delhi   Shanghai   Taipei   Toronto

With offices in

Argentina   Austria   Brazil   Chile   Czech Republic   France   Greece
Guatemala   Hungary   Italy   Japan   Poland   Portugal   Singapore
South Korea   Switzerland   Thailand   Turkey   Ukraine   Vietnam

Oxford is a registered trade mark of Oxford University Press
in the UK and in certain other countries

British Library Cataloguing in Publication Data
Data available

ISBN 978-0-19-917987-9

7 9 10 8

Available in packs
Stage 11 More Stories A Pack of 6:
ISBN 978-0-19-917983-1
Stage 11 More Stories A Class Pack:
ISBN 978-0-19-917990-9
Guided Reading Cards also available:
ISBN 978-0-19-917992-3

Cover artwork by Martin Remphry
Photograph of Susan Gates © Pauline Holbrook

Printed in China by Imago

Thud, thud, thud

My big brother's got some new trainers.
He wears them all the time.

Thud, thud, thud! When he runs
upstairs in them the whole house
shakes.

Mum shouts, 'Stop that noise!'

My brother's new trainers are big
and puffy and purple. They've got soles
as thick as tractor tyres.

Clump, clump. He's clumping to his bedroom.

'Gangway!' he shouts.

I have to squash myself against the wall, so my feet don't get crushed.

'I hate your horrible trainers!' I tell him. 'They're dangerous.'

But he just clumps downstairs again. *Thud, thud, thud.* The front door slams.

Thank goodness – he's gone out.

It's nice and peaceful now. I can lie here on the floor and read my book.

Stomp, stomp, stomp.

The floor begins to tremble.

Is a herd of elephants heading this way?

No, it's the new trainers. Here they come again – like great, purple, crushing machines.

'Mind my book. You're trampling on it!'

My big brother throws himself into a chair. He props his big purple feet up on one another.

'I can't see the telly now! It's my favourite programme. Your trainers are in the way!'

Mum says: 'Those new trainers are a menace! Take them off in the house!'

But my brother says, 'I love my new trainers. They're great! I'm never going to take them off! Not ever!'

'Then do up those dangly laces!' sighs Mum. 'You'll break your neck!'

But my brother just clumps outside. His long laces dangle behind him. And his monster trainers squash all the little daisies on the grass.

I hate those new trainers. They should be banned.

My brother even wants to go
to bed in his new trainers.

But Mum says: 'I've never heard of
anything so silly! Take them off!'

So he climbs up to his top bunk
bed. He throws down his new trainers,
whump, whump, so they land near
my bottom bunk bed.

Mum switches off our light.

I lie in the dark and watch the dangerous trainers.

They seem to be even bigger at night. They've got two big purple tongues that stick out at me and go, 'Ya boo!' They've got little eyes, like a spider.

The eyes are watching me back! The trainers are alive!

'Don't be silly,' I tell myself. 'Trainers can't be alive.'

I close my eyes so I can't see the trainers any more. Then I fall asleep.

But next morning, when I wake up, the trainers have moved! There's no doubt about it.

They're under my brother's computer desk now. And they're neatly side by side.

My big brother didn't move them because he's still in the top bunk, snoring.

'You've been out, haven't you?' I wag my finger at the trainers. 'When we were all asleep you went out on your own, didn't you?'

But the trainers don't say a word.

'Wait until tonight,' I warn them. 'I didn't see you go out last night because I fell asleep. But tonight I'll stay awake. I'll catch you, just wait and see.'

The top bunk's creaking. My big brother's waking up.

A life of their own

'Your trainers are alive,' I tell him.
'They go out at night on their own,
without you. You know those little
metal holes where you put your laces?
Well, they aren't lace holes. They're
eyes. Your trainers have got lots of eyes,
like spiders. Did you know that? And
they've got big slurpy purple tongues.'

But my brother just groans, 'You do talk a load of rubbish!' Then he turns over and goes back to sleep.

Those trainers are getting me really mad. They're wrecking my things. Today I found my crayons mashed into the carpet.

'You shouldn't have left them on the floor,' said my brother.

But I bet those trainers did it.

Clump, clump, clump. You can't get away from them. You can hear them all over the house.

'Who squashed this chewing gum into the carpet?' shouts Mum.

'It's these trainers,' says my big brother. 'I haven't got used to them yet. They're so big and heavy I can't control them. They keep treading on things!'

'Don't be silly,' says Mum. 'It's your fault, not your trainers. You're talking as if your trainers have a life of their own.'

Mum doesn't know it. But she's exactly right. Those trainers do have a life of their own. They have a secret life. They go out at night, on their own, when we're all asleep. They must do, mustn't they? How else could they be in a different place by morning?

Tonight I'm going to prove it. I'm going to follow those trainers and see where they go. I'm going to spy on them.

It's night time. It must be very late because the house is quiet. Mum and Dad are in bed. But I'm not asleep. I'm watching those trainers, like I said I would.

It's hard work. My eyes keep closing.

'Don't fall asleep!' I whisper to myself. 'Stay awake!'

The trainers are behaving themselves so far. They haven't moved at all. But their spider eyes are glittering in the dark.

I don't trust them. They're very sneaky. As soon as I close my eyes they'll be off, on their own.

But my eyelids are *so* heavy. My head is dropping down. ZZZZZZZZZZZZZZZ –

The trainers are on the move! I knew it! I knew they had a secret life.

They're marching down the stairs. *Clump, clump, clump.* What if they wake up Mum and Dad? But they don't. Even though they're making an awful din.

I slip out of bed and follow them. I tip-toe down the stairs in my bare feet.

At the bottom of the stairs the trainers stop. They look around.

'Ah ha,' I think. 'You're trapped now. The front door is locked.'

But the trainers aren't trapped. Have you ever seen a hamster squeeze through a tiny space? The trainers can do that. They squeeze, like purple toothpaste, through the letter box. First one, then the other.

Oh no, they're escaping. I look out
through the glass bit in the front door.
They're stomping down the garden path!

I turn the key in the front door and
let myself out. Mum would go mad if
she knew. It's very late. There's a big
silver moon in the sky. And I'm out here
in the garden, in my pyjamas.

But I'm on a mission. I'm finding out all about the secret life of trainers. I'm finding out what they do when we're all asleep.

I hide behind a bush and spy on them.

At first, they look very innocent.

They're walking around the garden in the moonlight. Just walking.

'That's not dangerous,' I think. 'They're just out for a walk, that's all. A walk in the moonlight.'

But no.

A moth flies by.

And suddenly, the trainers spring into action. One of them throws out a lace like a lasso.

Got it! The moth flutters. But it can't get free. Then the big purple tongue flicks out and, *gulp*, the moth is gone.

I can't believe it! The trainers aren't taking a walk. They're hunting. Hunting for things to eat. My brother's trainers are carnivorous!

They're very good hunters. They guzzle everything in sight.

A shiny black beetle trundles across the grass. He doesn't stand a chance. *Flick* goes the lace and he's dragged into the trainer's purple throat. *Crunch, crunch.*

'*Burp!*' goes the trainer.

A worm pops its head up. *Wham!* goes a trainer and stomps on it. The other trainer licks it up with its tongue.

The trainers sniff the air. They're looking for something else to gobble.

I hear a rustling in the bushes. A baby mouse pops out its pink nose. Oh no!

The trainers' eyes gleam at each other. They stay very, very quiet. They're waiting.

The baby mouse darts out of the grass.

'Run, mouse, run!' I shout. 'You're in deadly danger. The trainers will gobble you up! Run for your life!'

Leave them alone!

But the baby mouse doesn't hear me.
He doesn't know what danger he's in.
He doesn't know about the carnivorous
trainers.

He pitter-patters nearer, nearer. Fast
as you can blink, the laces flick out.
He's tied up like an Egyptian mummy!
A big purple tongue slides out and –

'Will you stop shouting?' says my
brother. 'I'm trying to get some sleep!'

I sit up in bed. 'I saw them. I saw your
trainers. They were out in the garden
hunting! They crunch beetles. They lick
up worms. They tied a baby mouse up
like a mummy!'

'What?' says my brother, rubbing his
eyes. 'Did you say a baby mouse?'

'Yes!' I cry. 'And I can prove it! Look,
they're not where you left them,
are they? They're in a
different place!'

My brother looks down from the top
bunk bed. The trainers aren't where he
threw them. They're neatly side by side,
next to the book case.

Mum switches on the light. 'What's
the matter? Who was shouting?'

'He was,' says my brother, pointing
at me. 'He's being silly, as usual. He
says he saw my trainers try to eat a
baby mouse. He says they've been out
in our garden hunting!'

'Well, why have they moved over there?' I shout at him. 'They weren't there when we went to sleep. That proves they've been out somewhere!'

'Oh, that,' says Mum. 'I moved them. I always come in when you're asleep and tidy up a bit. Haven't you noticed how this bedroom's always neat and tidy when you wake up?'

'No,' says my brother.

'But I saw them,' I tell Mum. 'I saw them out in the garden just now. They were munching a moth!'

'You just had a bad dream,' says
Mum. 'That's all.'

And she switches
off the light.

'Are you still awake?' I ask my
brother, in the dark.

'Yes,' comes a voice from the top
bunk.

'I did see them,' I tell him. 'Honestly,
it wasn't a dream. I should watch out if
I were you. I wouldn't put my feet in
those trainers. Not for a million pounds.
They might nibble your toes. They
might gobble your feet!'

'Just go to sleep,' says my brother.

But he sounds a bit worried.

The next day the house is very quiet. No *thud, thud*. No *clump, clump*. I can walk around in my bare feet. I can lie on the floor and read my book.

Where are the big, purple, mouse-guzzling trainers?

'I left them on the bus,' says my brother.

Mum goes mad. 'They were brand-new trainers. They cost a lot of money!'

'Sorry,' says my brother. 'It was an accident. Honest it was.'

Mum phones the bus company. Nobody's seen a pair of big, puffy, purple trainers with soles like tractor tyres.

'I can't understand it,' says Mum. 'There's no sign of them. They can't have walked off the bus by themselves!'

My brother and I look at each other. But we daren't grin because Mum's in a bad mood.

Keep your eyes open. One of these days, *you* might see a pair of big purple trainers. You might see them in the moonlight, clumping round your garden. You might hear a tiny *'Squeak, squeak!'* Then a *'Burp!'*

I'd leave them alone if I were you. I'd keep right out of their way.

And I wouldn't put my feet in them. Not even one little pink toe. Putting your toes inside a pair of carnivorous trainers could be very, very dangerous.

About the author

I have three children of my
own. They give me lots of
ideas for stories. Here's how
I got the idea for this story.
One day my big son, Alex,
bought a new pair of shoes.
They were enormous!
When he clumped around
in them the whole house shook.
Things got crushed beneath them – crayons,
books, fingers, toes – my little son,
Christopher, said 'Those are dangerous
trainers!' And I thought, 'Dangerous
Trainers? That's a good title for a story...'